Make-Believe Tales

UNICORNS
IN CHARGE

Written by Katherine Walker
Illustrated by Beverley Hopwood

make
believe
ideas

LETTER TO PARENTS

Dear Parents,

This book is an engaging early reader for your child.
It combines simple words and sentences with detailed
illustrations. Here are some of the many ways you can
help your child learn to read fluently.

Encourage your child to:
★ Look at and explore the pictures.
★ Sound out the letters in unknown words.
★ Read and reread the text.

Look at the pictures
Make the most of each page by talking about the pictures
and looking at their details together. Here are some questions
you can use to discuss each page as you go along:
★ What are the unicorns doing here?
★ How do you think the children feel here?
★ What different foods can you see on the table?
★ What's the cat doing in this picture?

Look at rhymes
Many of the paragraphs in this book are simple rhymes.
Encourage your child to recognize rhyming words.
Try asking the following questions:
★ What does this word say?
★ Can you find a word that rhymes with it?
★ Look at the endings of the rhyming words. Are they
  spelled the same? (Some are spelled the same, but not all.
  For example, "fun" and "sun," and "blue" and "flew.")

Test understanding

It is one thing to understand the meaning of individual words, but you want to make sure that your child understands whole sentences and pages.

★ Play "find the mistake." Read the text as your child looks at the words with you, but make an obvious mistake to see if he or she has understood. Ask your child to correct you and provide the right word.

★ After reading the story, close the book and make up questions to ask your child.

★ Ask your child whether an event did or didn't happen in the story.

★ Provide your child with two or three answers to a question and ask her or him to pick the correct one.

Sight words

This page provides practice with commonly used words that children need to learn to recognize on sight. Not all of them can be sounded out. Familiarity with these words will increase your child's reading fluency.

Picture dictionary

This activity focuses on learning vocabulary relating to the story. All the words can be found in the book.

Make-believe quiz

This simple quiz will help you ascertain how well your child has understood and remembered the text. If your child cannot remember an answer, encourage him or her to look back in the book to find out.

One spring day, our parents said,
"We've got to go away.
But while we're gone, we've called upon
the unicorns to stay."

GUESS WHAT!

Unicorns make great sitters. They are wise, caring, and lots of fun!

We ran outside to greet them.
Their coats were pink and blue.
Magic sprinkled from their wings,
and up and off we flew.

GUESS WHAT!

Unicorns come in every
color of the rainbow.

7

Our first stop was the playground,
to start the fun outside.
The unicorns used their magic horns
to make a rainbow slide.

GUESS WHAT!

Unicorns can make
rainbows of any shape
grow from their horns.

9

We visited the fountains.

The water shimmered like a jewel.

The unicorns flapped their pretty wings
to make a swimming pool.

GUESS WHAT!

Unicorns love a
pool party.

11

Dinner with the unicorns
was such a tasty spread:
rainbow pizza, fruit kebabs,
and yummy gingerbread.

GUESS WHAT!

Unicorn treats are magic.
They taste great, and they clean
your teeth at the same time.

The unicorns used their powers
to make our bath time fun.
They filled the tub with bubbles
that sparkled like the sun.

GUESS WHAT!

Unicorns can make sparkly bubbles with their horns.

The next day was a school day,
and we knew we wouldn't be late.
We soared above our classmates
and beat them to the gate.

GUESS WHAT!

Unicorns can fly
faster than birds.

After school was soccer,
and the unicorns joined in.
They're super skilled at scoring goals,
which helped our team to win.

GUESS WHAT!

Unicorns love team sports because they get to play with their friends.

Back home, we started crafting,
but we couldn't believe our eyes.
Our paper fairies came to life.
What a big surprise!

GUESS WHAT!

Unicorns make real creatures from their art projects.

23

When Mom and Dad were nearly home, we knew we had to clean. The unicorns swished their silky tails and made the house pristine.

GUESS WHAT!
Unicorns live in palaces that are always sparkly clean.

TOYS

Soon it was time to say goodbye,
and we felt a little sad.
But we had so many stories
to tell our mom and dad!

GUESS WHAT!

Every time you tell a story about a unicorn, their horn twinkles a little brighter.

27

SIGHT WORDS

Here are some sight words used in context. Use other sight words from the border in simple sentences of your own.

The unicorns love **to** cook.

They are good readers.

Unicorns **use** magic to clean **up**.

big ★ got ★ go ★ get ★ can ★ than ★ had

we ★ away ★ when ★ any ★ a ★ come ★ in ★ good ★ from ★ their ★ with

same ★ fun ★ them ★ were ★ so ★ was ★ our ★ came ★ make ★ day ★ at

like ★ you ★ off ★ soon ★ and ★ be ★ of ★ it

PICTURE DICTIONARY

Write the correct word under each picture to create your own picture dictionary.

fairy   dragon   wing
fountain   pizza   horn
unicorn   rainbow   bubble

MAKE-BELIEVE QUIZ

What have you learned about the unicorns from this story? Circle the correct answers. If you can't remember an answer, look back in the book.

1

At the playground, what did the unicorns make out of a rainbow?

a swing   **a slide**

2

What did the unicorns make for dinner?

burgers, fries, soda, and a salad

pizza, fruit kebabs, and gingerbread

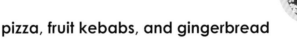

3

What special powers do unicorn treats have?

They clean your teeth.

They change flavor when chewed.

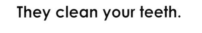

4

What sport did the unicorns play with the children?

soccer   **baseball**

5

How did the children get to school?

They rode the bus.

They rode the unicorns.

6

What are unicorn palaces like?

sparkly clean

dusty and dirty

7

What happens when you tell a story about a unicorn?

Its horn changes color.

Its horn twinkles brighter.

A DAY WITH THE UNICORNS

Take the quiz to find out how you would spend your perfect day with the unicorn sitters.

START

Do you prefer being inside or outside?

inside

outside

Do you like making things?

Are you happy to get your hands dirty?

yes

no

yes

no

You're going to tour a unicorn palace!

You're going camping with the unicorns!

Do you have a sweet tooth?

Do you love animals?

yes

no

yes

no

You're joining the unicorns for a fun day of crafting!

You're going on a unicorn photo safari!

You're taking a baking class with the unicorns!

You're taking part in the unicorns' field day!